KU-067-536

Contents

Introduction

William Makepeace Thackeray

Thackeray was born in 1811. As a child, he lived in India, where his father (like Jos Sedley in *Vanity Fair*) was a "collector", an officer who governed a large area for the British East India Company and collected its taxes.

Thackeray was sent to school in England in 1817. Then he went to Cambridge University. He did not complete his studies there, but he became the friend of some young writers and poets, including Edward Fitzgerald and Tennyson. He travelled in Europe, meeting the poet Goethe at Weimar. He began to study law in 1831, but he did not become a lawyer. Instead, he started to write for the newspapers. For a time, he also studied art in Paris.

He wrote for *Punch*, and his writing was directed more and more at the state of English society, especially the upper and middle classes. The *Punch* pieces that are probably best known today are "The Snobs of England" (1847), which showed the false pride and pretences of the people who wanted to seem important, the people who (like George Osborne's father in *Vanity Fair*) kept away from those they believed to be poorer or of a lower class than themselves. These pieces were gathered in a book, *The Book of Snobs*.

Thackeray attacks snobs and other people who have false pretences. His attacks are meant seriously, but they are not written like solemn judgements. He attacks with a laugh. He does not say that men like George Osborne are nasty. Instead we see George through Amelia's eyes as "the bravest and most beautiful man in the British army". And we learn that "it is possible that Lieutenant Osborne thought so too".

We learn about the people in *Vanity Fair* (1848), not so much by direct description as by Thackeray's smiling suggestions. For example, we build up our opinion of Becky Sharp, not from statements that she is a bad little creature, but from suggestions like this, when she is leaving Russell Square (pages 11–12):

> She took all the kind little Amelia's presents with just the right amount of unwillingness, and promised to love her friend for ever and ever ... As soon as she had said a very fond goodbye to Amelia, and had counted the gold coins that the kind Mr Sedley had put into a bag for her, and as soon as she had stopped drying the tears from her eyes (when the carriage had turned the corner), she began to wonder what a baronet would be like.

It is in fact Becky Sharp who makes us still enjoy *Vanity Fair* – making her way through the world with her clever plans, free from any control by conscience. When the story first appeared in monthly parts from 1847, Becky Sharp caught the public imagination. But Thackeray also gave his readers something new in his way of using the language: he seems to be *talking* to the reader; the story is addressed to a *listener*.

Thackeray continued to write short stories and novels like *Pendennis* (1848), *Henry Esmond* (1852), *The Newcomes* (1853–5) and *The Virginians* (1857–9). He died suddenly in 1863 from heart trouble.

Vanity Fair

In John Bunyan's *Pilgrim's Progress* (1678), the main character, Christian, had to pass through the town of Vanity, which had a market, "Vanity Fair", all through the year. This name *Vanity* reminded Bunyan's readers, and reminds us, of a text in the Bible, "Vanity of vanities ..." which is translated in the New English Bible as:

> Emptiness, emptiness, says the Speaker, emptiness, all is empty.   What does man gain from all his labour ... here under the sun? (Ecclesiastes 1:2)

Vanity Fair in *Pilgrim's Progress* is a place where they sell everything that is entirely without value – empty: fine houses, important positions, honours, titles, pleasures and delights of all kinds.

So the name of Thackeray's book tells us that the setting of his story is a world in which everybody is struggling to get things that are of no real importance.

When Thackeray wrote *Vanity Fair*, he was writing about a time which for him was not long ago.   In 1812, Napoleon Bonaparte had been forced, by the Russian winter, to turn back from Moscow.   He re-formed his armies, but they had to fight the armies of Prussia, Russia, Britain and Sweden.   At the battle of Leipzig in October 1813, the French were defeated by armies of twice their own numbers.   Napoleon's victorious enemies marched on Paris, and the emperor was sent to the island of Elba as its ruler.   In March 1815, Napoleon returned to France.   The war that ended in the battle of Waterloo in July 1815 forms the background of the first part of the story of *Vanity Fair*.

Chapter 1
Leaving school

There were two young ladies in the carriage that was leaving Miss Pinkerton's excellent school.

Amelia Sedley had a letter from Miss Pinkerton to Mr and Mrs Sedley. It said how much Amelia had learnt at the school, but it said more about the excellent education given at the school.

We are going to see a great deal of Amelia, so there is no harm in saying immediately that she was a dear little creature. As she is not a heroine, there is no need to describe her appearance. Indeed I am afraid that her nose was rather short, and her face was too round for a heroine. But she had a very nice smile, and her eyes were bright and happy-looking – except when they were full of tears, which was a great deal too often because she was the softest-hearted young lady in the world.

Just now, Miss Sedley could not decide whether to laugh or cry. She was glad to go home, but she was very sad about leaving her friends at school.

There was no letter from Miss Pinkerton about the other young lady in the carriage, Miss Rebecca Sharp.

Miss Sharp's father was an artist. He had taught drawing at Miss Pinkerton's school for young ladies. He was a clever man, good in company, especially in drinking company, and he was usually in debt. Rebecca's mother was French, a dancer in the theatre. She had had some education, and so Rebecca herself spoke perfect French as it is spoken in Paris.

Her mother, and then her father, died when Rebecca Sharp was seventeen. Miss Pinkerton, who had only

Rebecca and Amelia arrive home from school

seen her when she was behaving well, employed her at the school to speak French. For this she was given a few pounds a year, her bed and meals, and the chance to listen to the girls' lessons in her free time.

By the side of most of the older girls in Miss Pinkerton's school, Rebecca Sharp looked like a child. But she had already had a full education in the school of debt and need. She had learnt to turn from her father's door the many debt-collectors, the men who came to get money. She usually sat with her father and his friends, listened to their talk, and amused them with her own quickness of mind.

In the school, the only person Rebecca really liked was the gentle Amelia Sedley. So when Amelia left school at the age of seventeen, and Rebecca left to become a governess in Sir Pitt Crawley's family, they went together in the Sedleys' carriage. Rebecca was invited to stay with Amelia's family for a week before she went to begin her new employment.

By the time the young ladies reached the Sedleys' house in Russell Square, Amelia had dried her eyes and looked happy and excited. You may be sure she showed Rebecca every room of the house, and everything in all her cupboards, and her books, and her dresses, and her piano, and the two shawls that her brother Joseph had just brought her from India.

"It must be delightful to have a brother," said Rebecca rather sadly. "How you must love him! Isn't he very rich? They say all the men from India are rich."

"I believe he has plenty of money," Amelia answered.

Chapter 2
Joseph Sedley

When the dinner bell rang, the two young ladies went downstairs.

A very fat man was reading the newspaper by the sitting-room fire. He stood up quickly when the young ladies went in, and his face became very red.

"It's only your sister, Joseph," said Amelia. "I've finished school, you know. And this is my friend, Miss Sharp. You've heard me talking about her."

"No, never, really," said the fat man, shaking – "or rather, yes – what cold weather we are having, Miss!" And he attacked the fire to make it burn more brightly, although it was the middle of June.

"He's very good-looking," Rebecca whispered to Amelia. It was a rather loud whisper.

"Do you think so?" said Amelia. "I'll tell him."

"No! Please don't!" said Miss Sharp, stepping back like a frightened woodland creature.

Joseph Sedley was twenty-nine, twelve years older than his sister Amelia. He was in the East India Company's service, and at the time we are writing about, he was Collector of Boggley Wollah, an important position in Bengal. After twelve years at Boggley Wollah, hardly seeing another Englishman except twice a year (when the soldiers came to take the tax money to Calcutta) he became ill and had to return to Europe.

Before he went to India, Joseph was too young to enjoy the pleasures of a rich young man in London. Now he decided to enjoy them fully. He took rooms in a fashionable part of the town. He drove his horses in the park, he ate at the fashionable eating-houses, and he went to the theatres in the tightest of evening clothes. When he returned to India, he used to talk about this time in London as if he had been one of the leaders of fashion. But the truth is that he was as much alone in London as he had been at Boggley Wollah. He hardly knew anyone, and he had no company except his doctor and his illness. The sight of a lady frightened him, so that he seldom went to his family home in Russell Square.

At dinner, Amelia said to her brother, "Joseph, you haven't forgotten that you promised to take me to the Royal Gardens at Vauxhall, have you?"

"Good idea," said old Mr Sedley, "but the girls must have a gentleman each. Why not send to number ninety-six and ask George Osborne to join the party?"

I don't know why this made Mrs Sedley look at her husband and laugh. But Amelia looked down at the table, and her face was as red as only the face of a young lady of seventeen can be.

After dinner, Joseph found himself talking without fear to a young woman. Miss Rebecca asked him a great number of questions about India. They gave him a chance to tell her interesting stories about that country and himself. He told her about a tiger hunt, and his story frightened her.

"Oh, Mr Sedley," she said, "you must promise *never* to go on one of those dangerous tiger hunts again."

"You mustn't worry, Miss Sharp," he said, looking quite fearless. "The danger only makes the sport more exciting." He had only once been on a tiger hunt, when he nearly *was* killed – by fright.

Chapter 3
George Osborne and Dobbin

When Lieutenant Osborne came from 96 Russell Square to the Sedleys' house on the day of the Vauxhall party, he said to Mrs Sedley, "I hope you have room for Captain Dobbin of our regiment. I've asked him to come to dinner here and go with us to Vauxhall. I told him that Miss Amelia had come home."

"Of course," said Mrs Sedley. "But what an awkward fellow he is!"

"I don't care about Captain Dobbin's awkwardness," said Amelia with a smile. "I shall always like him, I know." Her reason, which she did not put into words, was that he was the friend of George Osborne, who was the most beautiful man in the British army and the most wonderful hero.

"There isn't a finer fellow in the army than Dobbin," Osborne said, "nor a better officer, though he isn't exactly good-looking." And he looked towards the looking-glass at himself with his splendid whiskers – and he saw Miss Sharp's green eyes watching him. And Rebecca thought in her heart, "Ah! I think I understand *you*, my fine fellow!"

That evening, when Amelia came into the sitting-room, singing like a bird and as fresh as a rose, she found a very tall, awkward-looking gentleman there. It was Captain William Dobbin of the Fortieth Regiment of Foot. If Amelia had known that he was there, she would never have come into the room singing. As it was, the sweet fresh little voice went right into the captain's heart. And that is a part of our story.

The party arrived at Vauxhall after dinner. As the splendid Jos stepped out of the carriage, the crowd gave a cheer for the "fat gentleman", who went rather red and looked very big and important, walking away with Rebecca. George, of course, took charge of Amelia.

"Look after the shawls and things, Dobbin," said George.

Of course our young people promised to keep together during the evening. And of course they separated in less than ten minutes. That always happens at Vauxhall. They would meet again at supper-time and discuss their adventures.

We won't follow any of them closely on those adventures. Mr Osborne and Miss Amelia were perfectly happy, seeing everything on the main walks in the gardens. Miss Rebecca Sharp and her overfed friend wandered into one of the side walks, as you might expect. The path was not well lit, and a careless passer-by caused Miss Sharp to fall back, with a little cry of fear, into the arms of Mr Sedley. That made him brave enough to tell her several of his India stories – for at least the sixth time.

"How I should like to see India!" said Rebecca.

"*Should* you?" said Joseph. And he was probably going to ask an even more daring question when (oh, how annoying!) the bell rang for the fireworks, and our interesting pair were forced to join the stream of people going to see the famous show of brightly coloured set pieces and noisy bursting rockets. One of the set pieces showed an unhappy Napoleon Bonaparte leading his army away from its defeat by the Russian winter.

Captain Dobbin did not find the Vauxhall amusements very amusing. He thought of joining the rest of his party

The party arrives at Vauxhall

at supper.   But he walked several times past the table where the other four had already met, and nobody took any notice of him.   The table was set for four people, and the four were talking quite happily.   Dobbin knew that he was completely forgotten.   He walked away, still carrying the young ladies' shawls.

Jos was enjoying himself, ordering the food and drink in a loud voice (and eating and drinking most of it himself).   At the end of the meal, he ordered a bowl of rack punch.   "Everybody has rack punch at Vauxhall," he said.   "Waiter!   Rack punch!"

That bowl of rack punch was the cause, I think, of all this history.   The young ladies did not drink it.   Osborne did not like it.   And the result was that Jos drank nearly all of it.   And the result of that was that he talked and laughed so loudly that a lot of people crowded round the table, laughing and cheering.

The ladies were very frightened, and Mr Osborne was very angry.

"Joseph," cried the lieutenant.   "Stop this, and let's go."   And the young ladies rose.

"Stop, my dearest, diddle-diddle-darling!" shouted Jos, now as brave as a lion, taking hold of Miss Rebecca.

Mr Osborne was getting ready to knock down a man who seemed to want to join Jos, when by good luck a gentleman who had been walking round the gardens arrived.   He pushed his way through the crowd, saying, "Go away, you fools!"   And he looked so fierce that the crowd disappeared.

"Where *have* you been, Dobbin?" said Osborne, taking Amelia's shawl from his friend's arm and putting it round that young lady's shoulders.   "You take charge of Jos, and I'll take the ladies to the carriage."

Chapter 4
The governess

Joseph Sedley did not appear at Russell Square the next day. But on the following day he sent a note to his sister:

> *Dear Amelia,*
> *I was too ill to come yesterday. I leave London today to take the water at Cheltenham. Please ask Miss Sharp to forgive me, if possible, for the way I behaved at Vauxhall. Ask her to forget every word I may have said when excited by that supper. As soon as I am better – my health has been greatly harmed – I shall go to Scotland for some months.*
>
> *Truly yours, Jos. Sedley*

Amelia wept, of course.

Rebecca did not weep. She took all the kind little Amelia's presents with just the right amount of unwillingness, and promised to love her friend for ever and ever.

She was to meet Sir Pitt Crawley at his town house in Great Gaunt Street and go with him to his country place, Queen's Crawley. The note about this had been written on an old envelope:

> *Great Gaunt Street*
> *Sir Pitt Crawley expecks Miss Sharp and baggidge to be here on Tuesday, as I leaf for Queens Crawley tomorro morning erly.*

Sir Pitt was a Knight Baronet. Rebecca had never seen a baronet, as far as she knew. As soon as she had said a very fond goodbye to Amelia, and had counted the gold coins that the kind Mr Sedley had put into a bag for

11

her, and as soon as she had stopped drying the tears from her eyes (when the carriage had turned the corner), she began to wonder what a baronet would be like. She expected to see him in fine clothes, perhaps with powdered hair.

In Great Gaunt Street, Sir Pitt's house had closed windows, not at all clean. Mr Sedley's driver rang the bell. The door was opened by a man in dirty old clothes, with a red face and smiling grey eyes.

"Is this Sir Pitt Crawley's?" the driver asked.

"Yis," said the man at the door.

"Take these bags in, then," said the driver.

"Take 'em in yourself."

"Don't you see I can't leave my horses? Come on and do your job, and Miss will give you some beer," said the driver, laughing because Miss Sharp had given nothing to the servants when she left the Sedleys' house.

The red-faced man took his hands out of his pockets, threw Miss Sharp's bags on his shoulder, and carried them into the house. Rebecca followed him in. When he put the bags down in the dining-room, she asked:

"Where is Sir Pitt Crawley?"

"Ha, ha! *I* 'm Sir Pitt Crawley. Don't forget you owe me some beer for bringing your bags in."

Rebecca, writing to Amelia from Queen's Crawley, described Sir Pitt as "an old, short, very dirty man in old clothes and farmer's boots, who smokes a very nasty pipe, and cooks his own nasty supper in a pan. He speaks like a farm-worker, and he uses some very bad language."

Sir Pitt himself may have had a taste for low life, but he was an important man at home and in the whole of Hampshire. When he drove out, four horses always pulled his carriage. In his dining-room, the food may have been very simple but there were always three men-servants to serve it.

Miss Sharp was to be governess to the two daughters of Sir Pitt by his second wife. By his first wife, he had had two sons. One of them was in the house, Mr Pitt Crawley, a very religious man. Rebecca described him to Amelia as "pale, thin, ugly, silent; he has thin legs, no chest, pale yellow whiskers and hair". His younger brother, Rawdon Crawley, was not in the house. He was never in the house when his brother was there because the two disliked each other very strongly.

Sir Pitt had an unmarried sister who was very rich. Because she was rich, she was treated with great honour when she visited Queen's Crawley. Sir Pitt had tried to get her to lend him some of her money, offering to pay two per cent interest. But she seemed to prefer to keep her money in five per cent government bonds. She had seventy thousand pounds.

Miss Crawley liked Sir Pitt's second son, who was not religious like his brother. She had paid Rawdon's debts more than once when he was at Cambridge and now that he was in the King's Dragoon Guards. And she let it be known that Rawdon Crawley would get a lot of her money when she died.

Now that we have met the more important members of the family, we must know something about Rebecca's duties in her new life. Her first duty, of course, was to make friends.

Sir Pitt's wife, Lady Crawley, was not important. No-body else in the house took any notice of her, so it was not necessary for Rebecca to make a friend of her.

It was not difficult to make the two girls like her. Rebecca did not worry them with too much learning. She let them educate themselves in the way they liked best. What education is better than self-education?

With Mr Crawley, Miss Sharp was quiet and serious. She used to ask him to explain parts of French books that she could not understand (although her mother was a Frenchwoman), and he was kind enough to choose serious books for her to read. He talked to her in the evenings on religious matters, often causing the tears to come to her eyes.

Mr Crawley was very pleased to be able to help her. "Miss Sharp is naturally good," he thought. "Her mother was a Montmorency, of course – one of the best families of France before the Revolution of 1789."

Indeed it was at Queen's Crawley that facts began to appear about Miss Sharp's family and its splendid past – before the Revolution destroyed all the best families in France. Before she had been in the house for more than a few months, she had several stories about her great family. Mr Crawley happened to find some of those stories in a book which was on the Queen's Crawley shelves, which showed that they were true.

Rebecca pleased her employer by reading all the law papers that came to him at Queen's Crawley. She helped him by copying many of his letters (and where necessary changing the spelling). She became interested in everything in and around Queen's Crawley, its park, its gardens, its animals. Soon the baronet hardly ever took his after-breakfast walk without her (and the children, of course). Before she had been a year at Queen's Crawley, she was almost wholly in charge of the house when Mr Crawley was away.

Chapter 5
Miss Crawley

It is time for us to meet Miss Crawley. She is coming to Queen's Crawley to visit her brother, Sir Pitt.

We already know the most important fact about this lady: she had seventy thousand pounds.

She disliked her older nephew, and when she came to Queen's Crawley, he soon went away on business.

Old Miss Crawley was not one of the women who were spoken of to Rebecca as Mr Crawley's idea of a good woman. She was not good. She had a nice little house in the most fashionable part of London, and she ate and drank far too much. She had a great deal of fun, and had been a beauty once, she said. (All old women were beauties once, we know.)

This splendid old lady was very fond of Rawdon Crawley. She paid for him to go to Cambridge, and when he was asked to leave the university after two years, she helped him to join the Dragoon Guards as an officer.

Rawdon led the life of a fashionable young "man-about-town". He hunted, played games, drove a four-horse carriage in races on the roads, and fought in the boxing ring. He was very fond of playing cards, and as a result of games of this kind he had fought three duels, showing clearly that he was not afraid of death.

"Or of what follows death, " Mr Crawley used to say.

Miss Crawley liked her favourite's bravery, and she always paid his debts after his duels. "A young man who *is* a man must often be in trouble, and he's worth twice as much as that soft goody-goody, his brother."

Rebecca wrote to Amelia:

Queen's Crawley has woken up. Miss Crawley has arrived with her fat horses, fat servants, fat little dog – the great rich Miss Crawley, with seventy thousand pounds in the five-per-cents. Our religious books are shut up, and Mr Pitt, whom she hates, has found it necessary to go to London.

The young man-about-town Captain Crawley has come. I suppose you want to know what he is like. Well, he is a very large young dragoon. He is two metres tall, and he speaks with a loud voice, and uses some very bad words. He shouts orders at the servants, but they all love him. When he has any money, he gives freely.

It was not long before Rebecca won the heart of that bad old woman, Miss Crawley.

One day, Sir Pitt had arranged a big dinner party and invited all the neighbouring baronets ...

"Not let Miss Sharp dine with us?" cried Miss Crawley. "Do you suppose I can talk about children with Lady Fuddleston, or law court business with that silly old Sir Giles Wapshot? No! I want Miss Sharp to be there. She's the only person I can enjoy talking to!"

So Miss Sharp the governess had orders to dine with the important people in the dining-room. And when Sir Giles had solemnly led Miss Crawley in to dinner, and was preparing to sit beside her, the old lady called out loudly, "Becky! Come and sit beside me and amuse me. Sir Giles can go and sit beside Lady Fuddleston."

When the party was over, and the carriages had rolled away, Miss Crawley said, "Come to my room, Becky, and we'll find fault with all the people who were at the party." And that is what the two new friends did perfectly.

"You funny, wicked little thing!" Miss Crawley said.

Miss Crawley

"You must sit beside me every day at dinner. And Rawdon will sit at my other side. I like him. I want him to run away with someone, you know."

"A rich someone, or a poor someone?"

"A rich girl, of course," said the old lady. "He has no money at all except what I give him, and he's in debt. He must get money and be a success in the world."

"Is he very clever?" Rebecca asked.

"Clever, my dear? He hasn't got an idea in his head except about his horses, his regiment, his hunting, and his card-playing. But he'll be a success because he's so delightfully wicked. Everybody in his regiment loves him."

Captain Crawley certainly enjoyed the company of Rebecca Sharp. His own talk was entirely right for a young officer of the Dragoons. Let us listen to them for a moment outside the house in the moonlight.

"Oh, what beautiful stars!" Miss Rebecca's eyes are turned up towards the sky, and the captain's are turned down towards her face. "I feel myself almost a spirit when I look up at them."

"Oh ... ah ... yes. So do I exactly, Miss Sharp... Er ... you don't mind my cigar, do you, Miss Sharp?"

Miss Sharp loves the smell of a cigar out in the garden more than anything else. She just tastes one, too, in the prettiest way possible – takes a little smoke into her mouth, gives a little cry, and a little laugh, and gives the precious thing back to the captain. He pulls at his whiskers and then at his cigar until the end is red and bright in the evening air. "Ah ... yes ... aw ... the finest cigar I ever smoked now ... aw." His mind and his talk are just what one expects from a dragoon.

Chapter 6
Amelia

Captain Dobbin went to the Sedleys' house in Russell Square. He had come to see whether George Osborne was there, of course. But he found only little Amelia, with a rather sad face, sitting near the window.

They talked about nothing at first. Then Amelia wanted to know if it was true that the Fortieth had received orders to leave England. The answer was, "No. Not yet."

Then: "Have you seen Lieutenant Osborne today?"

"I expect he's with his sisters," the captain said. "Shall I go and fetch him?"

So she gave him her hand gently and thankfully, and he crossed the square to the Osborne house.

Amelia waited and waited, but George never came.

Poor gentle little heart! And so it goes on, hoping and beating. It isn't much of a life to describe, is it? There isn't much happening. Only one feeling all day: "When will he come?" I believe George was playing billiards at the time when Amelia was asking about him. Because George was a cheerful fellow who loved company, and he was very good at games.

Amelia knew nothing about what was happening in Europe. Nothing, that is, until peace came to end the war – the war against Napoleon was over. Then her heart overflowed with joy: her hero was safe. Lieutenant Osborne's regiment would not have to go to fight. Amelia believed him to be the bravest and most beautiful man in the British army – in Europe – in the world. And it is possible that Lieutenant Osborne thought so too.

"What I want to know, George," old Mr Osborne said that evening – "What I want to know is, what is happening between you and that little Amelia Sedley?"

"Well, I ... ah ... I must say she's very fond of me. Anybody can see that."

"And you yourself?"

"Well, sir, didn't you order me to marry her, and don't I always obey you?"

The father did not look entirely pleased. "Yes. The marriage was agreed between Sedley and myself. But things change. It's true that Sedley helped me in my early days in business – helped me to gain success by my own hard work and cleverness. But I've thanked him enough for that. Between you and me, I don't like the look of Sedley's business. He has lost a ship and everything in it when an American warship attacked. And the end of the war in Europe hasn't been good for his business dealings. You can do better than marrying his daughter. Unless I see Amelia's ten thousand pounds marriage settlement on the table in front of me, you don't marry her. That's all."

When his father said "That's all", George knew he must not go on talking. He took the money order that old Mr Osborne had written, and left the room.

George Osborne changed the money order into bank notes the next day, paid Dobbin fifty pounds out of the money he owed him, and went to play billiards with some fellow officers. That same evening, Amelia wrote a long letter to him, full of love and fears, and hopes and anxieties.

"Poor little Emmy," George thought when he read it. "Dear little Emmy. How fond she is of me! – And what a headache that punch drink last night has given me!"

Chapter 7
Becky is married

Miss Crawley was ill. Captain Crawley of the Dragoon Guards rode to her London house in Park Lane on a splendid black horse.

The captain sent his name up, and Becky came down from the sick-room. She had come to London to look after Miss Crawley. She put a little hand in his and led him to the dining-room. And there, no doubt, they discussed the old lady's illness.

After that, the big dragoon came to the Park Lane house every day.

Very soon, Miss Crawley was so well that she sat up and laughed joyfully at Rebecca's perfect imitation of Miss Briggs, Miss Crawley's paid companion.

Soon after Miss Crawley got better, Lady Crawley, Sir Pitt's wife, died at Queen's Crawley. The news of her death caused very little sorrow at Park Lane. "I suppose I must tell my friends not to come to my party on Friday," said Miss Crawley. "I hope my brother won't be in a hurry to marry again."

"It will make Pitt very angry if he does," Rawdon laughed, showing his usual love for his brother.

Rebecca said nothing. She left the room before Rawdon went away, but they met again by chance near the front door and had a little talk.

The next day, Rebecca was looking out of Miss Crawley's bedroom window. She suddenly cried out, "Here's Sir Pitt!"

"My dear," said the old lady, "I can't see him. I won't

see him. Go downstairs and say I'm too ill to see any-one."

Rebecca ran lightly down the stairs in time to stop Sir Pitt from coming up. "She's too ill to see you, sir," she said.

"Oh, good!" Sir Pitt said. "It's *you* I want to see, Miss Becky. Come into the small sitting-room."

In the small sitting-room the baronet looked hard at her. "I want you back at Queen's Crawley," he said.

"I hope to come soon," Becky said in a low voice, "as soon as Miss Crawley is better – to return to ... to the dear children."

"You've been saying that for three months, Becky. And still you stay with my sister here. She'll throw you off like an old shoe when she has had enough of you. Will you come back? Yes or no?"

"I daren't – I don't think – it would be right – to be alone – with you, sir," Becky said.

"I say again, I want you." Sir Pitt struck the table. "I can't go on without you. The house all goes wrong; it isn't the same place. All my accounts are mixed up again. You *must* come back. Do come back! Dear Becky, do come."

"Come – as what, sir?" Becky's voice could hardly be heard.

"Come as Lady Crawley, if you like," the baronet said. "There! Will that be all right? Come back and be my wife. You're fit for it. You're as good a lady as I have ever seen. You've got more sense than any baronet's wife in Hampshire. Will you come? Yes or no?"

"Oh, Sir Pitt!" Rebecca was nearly in tears.

"Say yes, Becky. I'm an old man but a good one – good for twenty years more. I'll make you happy – I will!" And the old man went down on his knees.

Rebecca was almost unable to think. We have never seen her lose her self-control yet, but she did now, and wept some of the truest tears that ever fell from her eyes.

"Oh, Sir Pitt!" she said. "Oh, sir . . . I . . . I'm *married already.*"

It just happened that Miss Briggs was outside the door of the small sitting-room during most of this talk. When Sir Pitt Crawley fell on his knees, she ran to Miss Crawley and told her.

The old lady arrived in a hurry.

"He isn't on his knees at all," she said angrily to Miss Briggs. And to Sir Pitt she said, "What's this about your offering to marry my little friend? It isn't true, is it?"

"Yis," said Sir Pitt.

"I have thanked Sir Pitt Crawley," Rebecca said, "and I have told him that . . . that I can never become Lady Crawley."

"Refused him!" Miss Crawley couldn't understand.

"Yes – refused," said Rebecca sadly.

The old lady turned to Sir Pitt. "And did you really offer to marry her?"

"Yis."

"And she refused you?"

"Yis." There was a cheerful smile on the baronet's face.

Miss Crawley didn't know what it was all about. A rich old gentleman of high position offers marriage to a penniless governess, and then laughs when she refuses! A penniless governess refuses an offer of marriage from a baronet with four thousand pounds a year! It was a complete mystery.

It was Miss Briggs who learnt the truth about the marriage in a letter from Becky. She went to give the news to Miss Crawley.

"Where's Becky?" the old lady asked.

"She's gone away. She's married to——"

"Married! Who is she married to? Come on! Speak!" Poor Miss Briggs. She was shaking with fear as she said: "To – a member of the family."

"*Who?* She refused Sir Pitt. *Who?*"

"She's married to ... to Captain Rawdon Crawley."

"Rawdon married?" cried the old lady. "Rawdon – Rebecca – governess – nobody! Get out of my house, you fool, you stupid old Briggs! How dare you?" And Miss Crawley fell back.

They sent for the doctor.

When Sir Pitt Crawley heard that Rebecca's husband was his son, his language was terrible – not the kind of language we can have on these pages. It sent poor Briggs running out of the room, white-faced. And with her we will shut the door on the sight of the madly angry, unhappy old man.

"Suppose the old lady doesn't forgive us," Rawdon said to his little wife as they sat in their nice little rooms near the Dragoons' quarters. The new rings looked lovely on her little hands. The new shawl was beautiful. And the new watch ticked quietly over her heart. "Suppose she doesn't forgive us, eh, Becky?"

"Then *I'll* make us rich," she said.

"Of course," he said, kissing her little hand. "You can do anything. And we'll drive down to the Star and Garter Hotel and have dinner there, won't we?"

Chapter 8
Amelia is married

You would hardly know the house in Russell Square. It was so changed, with all the furniture moved, and with numbers stuck on everything.

You would know just one of the many people in the house: Captain Dobbin. He was interested in one thing that was being sold: a small square piano. Nobody else was interested in it, and he got it for twenty-five pounds.

John Sedley's business had failed (as old Mr Osborne expected), and his house and everything in it was being sold. Napoleon had landed at Cannes, and the news destroyed the business, and with it the family.

The piano had been Amelia's, and she might need one now. Indeed it arrived that evening at a pretty little cottage in Chelsea, to the west of London.

As you would expect, Jos Sedley wrote to his mother – he did not come to London – telling her to draw as much money as was needed from his bankers. So his old parents had no need to be afraid of being poor. Jos himself stayed at Cheltenham, driving his light carriage, eating and drinking, and telling his stories about India.

Most people in the business houses of London soon forgot John Sedley. A few wanted immediate payment of his debts. The most cruel seemed to be John Osborne, his old friend and neighbour – John Osborne, who owed all his success to Sedley, and whose son was to marry Sedley's daughter. These things all explain Osborne's wish to hurt the Sedleys.

He wrote a short note to Amelia, telling her that

all arrangements between her and Lieutenant George Osborne were over.

A few days afterwards, Dobbin found Osborne in his room in the quarters of the Fortieth Regiment.

"Look, Dobbin. She's ... she's sent back everything I ever gave her." There was a small parcel with a ring, a silver knife that he had bought her when he was a boy, a gold chain, and other inexpensive things. And there was a letter in the well-known, rather childish writing:

My father has ordered me to return these presents to you. And I must not write to you again after this. Goodbye. I pray to God to keep you safe.

I shall often play on the piano – your piano. It was like you to send it. Thank you and bless you.

Captain William Dobbin didn't know how it happened, but he found himself the arranger of the marriage between George Osborne and Amelia. It was about the most painful thing he had ever done. But when he had a duty to do, Captain Dobbin always did it. When he found Miss Sedley at the little cottage in Chelsea, she was dying of sorrow. When he brought George to her, she changed. She grew young again, laughed and sang.

Dobbin left them together.

A much harder heart than George Osborne's would have been softened by such selfless love as Amelia's. To be able to bring happiness to her so easily gave him a sense of power. His father had forbidden him to see her again, but – as Dobbin showed him – when the regiment went to war, old Mr Osborne would forgive him.

Jos Sedley was at the church for the marriage of George and Amelia. He was splendid. He was fatter than ever.

George and Amelia are married

The time came for George and Amelia to promise to be true to each other until death separated them. Osborne's "I will" came in a strong, deep, manly voice. Emmy's "I will" came from her heart, but hardly anybody heard it – except Captain Dobbin.

For the first few days after their marriage, George and Amelia had chosen Brighton, the fashionable seaside town on the south coast. They had rooms at the Ship Hotel, and they enjoyed themselves there quietly.

After a time, Jos joined them. And he was not the only friend they found there. As they came back to the hotel from a seaside walk one afternoon, they met Rebecca and her husband. Rebecca flew into the arms of her dearest friend. Crawley and Osborne shook hands.

There was plenty to talk about. Dobbin had agreed to tell George's father about the marriage, and young Osborne was rather worried about the possible result. Miss Crawley had refused to see Rawdon and Becky at Park Lane, and they had followed her to Brighton to try to see her. Miss Crawley had come to Brighton for a rest after her illness.

There was another reason for Rawdon and Becky to leave London and take the best rooms at the best hotel in Brighton. They had no money. Not that one needs real money in Vanity Fair. But dealing with debt-collectors is tiring, and Becky wanted a rest.

Rawdon, with shouts of laughter, told several amusing stories about Rebecca's clever way of treating debt-collectors. The four friends often spent the evening together. After two or three nights, the gentlemen played a few games of cards while their wives sat and talked. Then Jos arrived in his grand open carriage, and he played a few games of billiards with Captain

Crawley. These games of cards and billiards put a little ready money into Rawdon's pocket.

One evening, the three gentlemen walked down to see the Lightning coach come in from London.

"Hullo! There's old Dobbin," George cried.

Dobbin had promised to visit them at Brighton. He was sitting on the roof of the coach, and he waved and climbed down. Osborne took him to one side. "What's the news?" George asked. "Have you seen my father? What does he say?"

Captain Dobbin looked serious. "I've seen your father," he said. "How's Amelia – Mrs George? I'll tell you all the news in a minute. But I've brought the greatest news of all! We're to go to Belgium. The whole army goes, including the Guards."

This news of war caused the three men to look very serious.

Later that evening Captain and Mrs Crawley discussed the news.

"I say, Becky, what'll Mrs O do when O goes out with the regiment?"

Becky answered, "I suppose she'll cry her eyes out."

"*You* don't care, I suppose?"

"You wicked man! Don't you know that I'm coming with you? Besides, you're different. You're going to be General Tufto's staff officer. *We* don't fight in a line regiment." And that pleased her husband so much that he had to kiss the proud little head.

"Rawdon, dear," she said after a moment. "Don't you think it would be ... er ... wise to get the money he owes you from George, before he goes?"

Chapter 9
Brussels

Amelia did not cry her eyes out. The army was going to Belgium, but nobody expected battles. All sorts of people besides the army were going to Brussels and Ghent. It was like going to a great party. Amelia decided to go too. Jos agreed to go with her and look after her when George was away with his regiment.

The weeks that followed in Brussels were such an exciting part of Jos's life that it gave him something to talk about for years after. His tiger hunt story was put aside, and its place was taken by far more exciting stories that he had to tell about adventures before, during and after the great battle of Waterloo.

For a few weeks, Amelia was truly happy. George took her to a new entertainment every evening – and was quite pleased with himself for doing so. Then they were riding in the park one day when George said, "That's General Tufto, who has command of the Third cavalry division. That means that the Crawleys are here."

Amelia's heart fell – she didn't know why. The sun didn't seem to shine so brightly.

George Osborne was right. The next day, they saw a small group of the greatest men in Brussels. In the middle of the group was Rebecca, wearing the prettiest riding clothes and riding a beautiful little horse. Rebecca waved two or three fingers playfully at Amelia, but Rawdon rode over and shook hands with Amelia and Jos.

After they had seen the great men in the park, there was plenty for Amelia, Jos and George to talk about until it was time to go to the theatre. There George had to go and speak to Rebecca Crawley where she sat between General Tufto and Rawdon.

And so it went on, day after day, until the evening of the great dance.

George got tickets for the dance from Rebecca. And so it was natural for him to leave Amelia on a seat in a corner while he went to thank Mrs Crawley. It was there that Rebecca herself found Amelia, alone and unhappy.

"Look, Amelia, " Rebecca said, "you must stop George from playing for money. He and Rawdon play cards every night, and you know Rawdon will win every penny from him. Why don't you stop him?"

Rebecca couldn't say more to her dear friend because, of course, George soon found her.

"Have you come to take me away to dance?" she said. And she left her shawl and her flowers with Amelia and went away with George. Amelia sat there, alone, and waited for the end of the evening.

At last George came back for Rebecca's shawl and flowers. Mrs Crawley was going away. George took the flowers to her, and Becky's eyes immediately saw the note among them. She was used to receiving notes now. She gave George a quick, knowing smile and walked away.

George was so excited that he forgot Amelia – Dobbin found her and took her to her hotel. George went to a play table and – it seemed to be his lucky night – won quite a lot of money. Dobbin found him and led him away.

"The enemy has crossed the Sambre River," said Dobbin, "and the left of our army is already fighting. Come on We are to march in three hours."

George went quietly to his hotel bedroom. The night-light showed him Amelia's sweet, pale face. She seemed to be sleeping.

"How pure she is!" he thought. "How gentle! And how friendless! How bad a husband I have been!" He wished undone all the wrong that he had done her, though he knew he could not change the past.

He bent silently towards the gentle pale face. Two soft white arms closed lovingly round his neck. "I'm awake, George," the poor child said. At that moment the drums began to sound. The whole city woke.

We must see some of the other people who will remain in Brussels while the army marches away. One of them, of course, was Jos. He was asleep when Dobbin found time for a quick visit.

"You're going to look after your sister, aren't you?" the captain asked. "If anything happens to George, remember she has no one except you to take her safely back to England. And if we suffer a defeat——"

"Defeat?" Jos thought the captain might not be so brave as everyone said he was. "Defeat? Impossible, sir! But of course I'll look after her."

"Look," Rawdon said. "If I'm hit, Becky, let's see what there is for you. I've had some quite good luck here, and there's two hundred and thirty pounds of winnings. I won't take either of my own horses: they ought to be worth something. Your little horse that the general gave you will sell for quite a lot." And he went on naming things that Rebecca could turn into money. He put on his oldest army clothes, and then he took his little wife up in his arms and held her against his heart for a minute.

When he put her down, there were tears in his eyes.

When he had gone, Becky took off the pink dress she had worn at the dance. A piece of paper fell out of it. She picked it up with a smile, and locked it in her dressing-box. Then she had some coffee and continued Rawdon's examination of things she owned. She had quite a lot of jewels besides those that Rawdon had given her. Among other things, there were two little gold watches covered with jewels; General Tufto had given her one, and the other was a present from George Osborne. If the worst happened, Mrs Rawdon Crawley would not do badly.

When Jos heard the guns from Quatre Bras, he was frightened and wanted to leave Brussels. But everyone was going, and he could find no horses.

"Do you know where I can get horses?" he said, when he happened to meet Rebecca.

"You're not going, are you? Who's going to look after Amelia, that poor little sister of yours? You're not leaving her?"

"I won't leave her," cried the frightened Collector of Boggley Wollah. "There's a seat for her in my carriage, and one for you, dear Mrs Crawley, if you will come – and if we can get horses!"

"I have two horses to sell," the lady said.

Jos nearly kissed her.

They started to talk about the price. Jos never spent a half-hour in his life which cost him so much money. But at last the business was finished.

The noise of gunfire from Quatre Bras had lasted for only six hours. But Jos was glad he had the horses. Perhaps the story was true that the French under Marshal

Ney had been defeated, but there was still the main French army under Napoleon himself.

Much louder than the guns of Quatre Bras, the guns of Waterloo began their terrible noise.

It was too much for Jos. "I can't bear it any more, Emmy," he said. "I won't bear it. And you must come with me."

"Without my husband?" Amelia said with a look of wonder.

Jos really could not bear it any more. "Goodbye, then!" he said, and he ran out to his carriage.

All that day, from morning until after sunset, the guns roared. It was dark when the gunfire suddenly stopped. Everybody knows the history of that day. All day long, the English regiments of foot soldiers stood and received the attacks of the French cavalry. Shot, from the guns that could be heard in Brussels, tore through their lines. Men fell, and the rest closed in. Towards evening, the attack of the French slowed down. At last, their finest regiments, the Imperial Guard, marched up the hill into the mouths of the English guns. On and up they came. They were nearing the top of the hill when the gunfire became too much for them. The attacking lines stopped, still facing the terrible guns. Then at last the English left the hilltop that they had defended so fiercely.

Still in their lines, they came down the hill towards the French, and the Guard turned and ran back.

No more gunfire was heard at Brussels. The fighting rolled far away. Darkness came down on the field and the city. And Amelia was praying for George, who was lying on his face, dead, with a bullet through his heart.

English soldiers at the battle of Waterloo

Chapter 10
Paris and London

A few weeks after the battle of Waterloo, a parcel arrived at Brighton for Miss Crawley. That lady had already seen in the newspapers the news about her nephew's bravery at Waterloo and his being made a colonel. The parcel contained presents and a letter from Rawdon.

The presents were parts of the sword and marks of rank of a high officer of the French Imperial Guard. The letter told Miss Crawley, in an amusing way, how Rawdon got these things on the field of battle.

"Of course, I know," Miss Crawley explained to Miss Briggs, "that Rawdon couldn't write such a good letter. It's that clever little creature that tells him what to say."

She was right, of course. Becky did write the letter. But did Miss Crawley know that Becky also bought the presents from one of the market people in Brussels, who were very soon selling every kind of souvenir from the battlefields?

Becky and Rawdon spent the winter of 1815 in Paris. The price poor Jos Sedley had paid for the two horses made it possible for them to live well.

Becky's success in Paris was surprising. All the French ladies liked her. She spoke their language very well. The gentlemen were delighted with her as she rode in the Bois de Boulogne. At her parties, the most famous people from Prussia, Russia, Spain and England tried to get near the amusing little lady. Paris was full of great men and women, and most of them knew the delightful Mrs Rawdon Crawley. She moved among the most

Becky and Rawdon enjoy themselves in Paris

fashionable people as if she had been born among them.

General Tufto was not very happy. Mrs Tufto had come to Paris. And besides, there were a lot of other generals round Mrs Crawley's chair or carriage. But Rawdon was enjoying himself. There were no debt-collectors in Paris yet. There was plenty of card-playing, billiards and other games, and Rawdon's luck was good.

On the twenty-sixth of March 1816, Rebecca had a son. When Miss Crawley read about this, she was angrier than we have yet seen her.

The old lady ordered her nephew Pitt to come immediately to Brighton. And she told him that he must marry her niece, Lady Jane, the daughter of Lord and Lady Southdown, at once. Both Pitt and Lady Jane were good. They always obeyed their parents and Miss Crawley. Miss Crawley also promised them money: she would give them one thousand pounds a year while she was alive; and they would get most of her money and other possessions when she died.

So Lady Jane became Lady Jane Crawley.

Old Miss Crawley wanted to punish the nephew who had been her favourite before. But she made a mistake. She ordered Pitt and Lady Jane to come and live with her. The result, which she did not expect, was that Lady Jane's very strong-minded mother, Lady Southdown, continued her command of the good Lady Jane in her new home. Lady Southdown took command of the whole house. She pitilessly forced her medicines and religious books on everybody in the house, including Miss Crawley. She was so strong-minded that Miss Crawley lost her control of her own house. She grew so frightened that she even stopped being unkind to Miss Briggs.

The poor old lady was so afraid of Lady Southdown that she became more and more fond of Lady Jane (because we must remember that she never really liked Lady Jane's husband). Let's hope that the kind-hearted Lady Jane helped the frightened old lady and led her gently out of the busy struggle of Vanity Fair. We shall not see Miss Crawley again.

Rawdon Crawley and his wife lived very happily and comfortably in Paris for two or three years. Rawdon had left the Dragoon Guards, though he still kept the title "Colonel" before his name. He and Becky had therefore no income at all.

Their friends, enjoying the very good dinners that Mrs Crawley's servants brought to the table, wondered how it was possible to live so well on an income of nothing a year. We, of course, know that it is perfectly possible to live well on nothing a year in Vanity Fair.

Colonel Crawley played so much billiards and so many games of cards that he became a complete master. Like a great general, his skill became greatest when he was in most danger. When the luck had not been on his side for almost a whole game of billiards, he might seem certain to lose both the game and his money. That was when the man who was winning, and his friends, offered to increase the amount of money hanging on the result. And that was when Colonel Crawley showed what a great player he was. Two or three wonderful hits brought victory to him, to the surprise (and cost) of the losers. The same thing happened at cards.

Rawdon's winnings certainly helped, but the Crawleys were living so well that they found it necessary to owe quite a lot of money. A few of the people to whom debts were owed may have begun to be anxious. But just at this time, there came from England some news that made their anxiety much less. Mrs Crawley made sure that the news spread.

Colonel Crawley had a very rich aunt, Miss Crawley. He expected to receive a great deal of money when she died, and the news was that Miss Crawley was dying. The great colonel had to hurry away to her bedside. Mrs Crawley was to remain in Paris until he came back.

He went to Calais, and it was supposed that he had gone by ship to England. But instead he went to Brussels. He liked Brussels. The fact is, he owed more money in London than in Paris.

The aunt, Miss Crawley, was dead, Paris learnt. Mrs Crawley dressed herself and little Rawdon in black clothes. The colonel, Paris understood, was arranging the business of his new riches. The Crawleys would be able to move to the first floor of the hotel instead of the less expensive rooms they had been using. Mrs Crawley and the hotel owner had a friendly discussion about the new curtains and furniture for the first floor rooms, and soon settled everything – except the bill.

"Look after my bags and boxes very carefully, won't you?" she said to the hotel owner.

He put the things into his store-room. (When he opened them, months later, there was nothing of special value in them.) And she went away in one of his carriages, her French maid with her, and her child by her side.

Before she went to Brussels to join her husband, Mrs Crawley made a visit to London. She left little Rawdon with the maid in France. Saying goodbye did not cause either Rebecca or her son much pain. Indeed, neither of them had seen much of the other since Rawdon was born. He had been nursed in a village near Paris. His father often rode there to visit him, and was very pleased to see him pink-faced and dirty, shouting happily and playing in the rich black soil with other children.

It was not for some weeks after the Crawleys' departure that the hotel owner found out what had happened to him. He found it out after the hat-maker had visited the hotel several times with her bill for things supplied to Mrs Crawley, and after the jeweller from the Palais Royal had asked a number of times if the *charmante* lady was back, because she had forgotten to pay for a good many watches and things. The hotel owner himself hated the whole English nation from that time on.

The purpose of Rebecca's visit to London was to reach a kind of settlement with the many people her husband owed money to. By getting them to take a small part – say ten per cent – of the amount of the debt as full payment, she would make it possible for him to return home.

"That's all the money he has. My husband would really prefer to stay in Europe rather than come to live in England with his debts not settled ... No, there is no money coming to him from anywhere else ... No, you will never get a larger amount than I am offering ..."

With arguments like these, the clever little woman made the people who were owed money take fifteen hundred pounds of real money in settlement of ten times that amount of debts.

And so, Colonel and Mrs Crawley came to London. And it was at their house in Curzon Street, Mayfair, that they really showed the skill which is necessary for anyone who wants to live on an income of nothing a year.

Chapter 11
Widow and mother

When the news of George's death came to the Osborne family, his sisters cried aloud in their sorrow. But it was worse for George's old father. You remember that Dobbin had gone to see old Osborne after the marriage of George and Amelia. George's father had gone nearly mad. He was so angry that he swore to forget that George had ever been his son. His lawyer had sent George the two thousand pounds that his mother had left for him, and had added:

Mr Osborne orders me to say that he will not receive any messages, letters, visits or other communications from you. You are not, from now on, his son.

Old Osborne tried to tell himself that George had died on the field of battle as a punishment for disobeying his father. He tried to put all the blame on Amelia. If she had died, instead of George, father and son could have met again, and he could have forgiven the boy.

Three weeks after Waterloo, Mr Osborne got a letter that George had written before the battle.

We march in an hour for a great battle. So I want to say goodbye to you. And I ask you to be good to the wife – perhaps also the child – I may leave. I am afraid I have already wasted a large part of the money my mother left. Thank you for all your kindness to me in the past. I promise that, whether I fall in the field of battle or live through it, I shall do so in a way that will make you proud of me. George

George's pride, or perhaps awkwardness, had prevented him from saying more. The broken-hearted old gentleman read the letter twice, then dropped it with the most terrible mixed feelings of love and hatred. His son was still loved and not forgiven.

Towards the end of October, Osborne told his daughters that he was going overseas. He did not say where he was going, but they knew he was going to see the place where George had died. They also knew that George's widow, Amelia, was still in Brussels.

As Osborne drove in a carriage towards Brussels after seeing the battlefield, another carriage came in the opposite direction. There was a lady in the carriage. And riding beside it was an officer.

It was Major Dobbin. Mr Osborne sat back quickly.

The lady in the carriage was Amelia. But how changed she was from the fresh young girl Osborne remembered. Her face was white and thin. Her eyes were fixed and looking nowhere. They stared straight at Osborne as the carriages passed each other, but she did not know him. Nor would he have known her if Dobbin had not been beside the carriage.

The old man hated her. He did not know how much he hated her until he saw her there.

"Mr Osborne!" cried Dobbin, as he rode up and held out his hand.

Osborne did not take the hand. He shouted to the driver to hurry on.

Dobbin put his hand on the side of the carriage. "I will see you, sir," he said. "I have a message for you."

"From that woman?" asked Osborne fiercely.

"No. From your son."

"What do you want to say to me, Captain Dobbin? Or I ought to say *Major* Dobbin, better men than you being dead so that you take their place!"

"Better men *are* dead," Dobbin replied. "I want to speak to you about one."

"Be quick, then," said Osborne, looking angry.

Dobbin didn't allow himself to be angry. "I was his closest friend," he said, "and he told me his wishes before we went into action. Do you know how little money his widow has?"

"I don't know his widow. Let her go back to her father."

Dobbin's self-control was excellent as he said: "Do you know Mrs Osborne's condition, sir? Her life and indeed her mind have been shaken by the terrible thing that has happened to her. The doctors are very anxious about her, but there is one chance left, and that is what I came to speak to you about. She will be a mother soon. Are you going to punish the child because the father disobeyed you? Or will you forgive your son's child?"

Osborne broke out into a wild mixture of explanation and blame. "No father in England was ever kinder to his son than I was to George. And how does he repay me? By disobeying my clear order. He died without even telling me he was wrong. He brought his punishment on his own head. I am a man of my word, and I promise you that I will never speak to that woman. Nor will I allow that she is my son's wife. *And that's what you may tell her!*"

There was no hope there, then.

A day came when the poor widow pressed a child to her – a child with the eyes of George – a little boy – as beautiful as could be. How she laughed and wept over it!

She was safe. The doctors saw that the danger to her life and to her mind had passed.

It was Dobbin who brought the mother and child home to England and to her parents' house. And it was Dobbin who went very often to the little house in Chelsea and spent hours talking to the Sedleys and Amelia.

One day, Dobbin arrived in a carriage, bringing a wooden horse, a drum, and other warlike toys for little Georgy – who was hardly six months old.

"I've come to say goodbye, Amelia," said the major, taking the little white hand gently.

"Goodbye? And where are you going?" she said.

"If you send letters to the London agents of the regiment, they will send them to me – because you *are* going to write to me, aren't you? I'll be away a long time."

"I'll write to you about Georgy," she said. "Dear William, how kind you have been to him and to me. Look at him. Isn't he wonderful?"

The little pink hands of the child closed round the honest soldier's fingers, and Amelia looked up into his face with the proud happy look of a fond mother. That smile wounded him more than the cruellest look could have done. He bent over mother and child. He could not speak for a moment. And it was only with all his strength that he could force himself to say, "God bless you."

"God bless you," said Amelia, and held up her face and kissed him. "Hush! Don't wake Georgy!" she added, as William Dobbin went to the door with heavy steps. She didn't hear the noise of his carriage wheels as he drove away: she was looking at the child, who was laughing in his sleep.

Chapter 12
How to live well on nothing a year

It is necessary, if you are to live on nothing a year in Vanity Fair, to have a house.

Colonel and Mrs Crawley could not buy a house in London, so they looked for a house to rent in a fashionable part of the town.

At one time, Mr Raggles was the butler in Miss Crawley's house. Mrs Raggles had been a cook in the same house. The butler's pay had been good, and it had been possible for him to get and save money in other ways. The cook had left her employment and opened a small fruit and vegetable shop not far from Miss Crawley's Park Lane house. In time, Mr Raggles left Miss Crawley's service. Then to the things they sold in the little shop they added milk, cream, butter, eggs and other simple foods fresh from the country. They knew very many of the butlers in that part of London, and they had a very comfortable back room where Mr and Mrs Raggles received them. So they were soon supplying milk, cream, butter and eggs to more and more houses.

Year after year, the Raggles's savings increased until they were able to buy the house and furniture of 201 Curzon Street. It is true that Mr Raggles had to owe some of the money to a friend at rather high interest (about fifteen per cent), but most of it came from his own savings.

Mr and Mrs Raggles did not intend to live in such a splendid house. But it was quite easy to find rich people who wanted to rent it.

Mr Raggles was a good man – good and happy. The

house brought him such a good income that he decided to send his children to really good and expensive schools. He had been born at Queen's Crawley, the son of a gardener there, and he loved the Crawley family. It happened that Raggles's house in Curzon Street was empty when Rawdon and his wife returned to London. The old man was glad that a member of the family was to rent his house.

Old Mr Raggles not only let the colonel rent 201 Curzon Street. He acted as the butler whenever the Crawleys gave a dinner party. And Mrs Raggles came into the kitchen and sent up to the dining-room dinners that old Miss Crawley herself would have been proud of.

This, then, was the way Crawley got his house for nothing. It is true that Raggles had to pay the taxes, the interest on the money he still owed for the house, the insurance, the cost of food and drink for his family – and for a time for the colonel – the cost of school for his children, and other expenses. It is true that the Raggles's happy life was entirely destroyed by the Crawleys' use of his house, Raggles himself being sent to prison for debt. But *somebody* has to pay, even for gentlemen who live on nothing a year.

The dinners at 201 Curzon Street were wonderful and always cheerful. The sitting-rooms were very pretty, with a thousand little objects that Rebecca had brought from Paris. And when Rebecca sat down and sang at the piano, the visitors thought that everything was delightful. Perhaps the husband was rather stupid, but his wife was the pleasantest little lady in London.

Very soon, rich and powerful men began to enjoy visits to Curzon Street. Men of fashion surrounded

Rebecca's carriage in Hyde Park. But notice that the word is "men". The ladies kept away. Some of them pretended not to see her, and others looked in the opposite direction when they passed.

At first, Rawdon was very angry when the ladies were not polite to his wife. He wanted to make their husbands fight a duel with him.

"No," said Rebecca. "You can't *shoot* me into the best circles, Rawdon dear. Remember that I was only a governess, and you, you poor foolish old man, have a terrible name for debt, games of chance, duelling, and all kinds of wickedness. We'll get as many friends as we want after a time, but you will have to be a good boy and obey your teacher in everything she tells you to do."

"I'll be good," Rawdon said. "Without you, I'd be in prison in Paris for debt. You clever little darling!"

Late one night, a party of gentlemen were sitting round the sitting-room fire in the Crawleys' house.

"Rawdon," said Becky, "I must have a sheepdog."

"A what?" said Rawdon, looking up from the card table. Usually he gave all his attention to his game of cards, and didn't join in the talk except when it was about horses and racing.

"What *can* you want a sheepdog for?" asked young Lord Southdown. "You haven't got any sheep."

"I mean a dog to look after *me*, to keep the wolves off me," said Becky, laughing and looking up at Lord Steyne.

The great Lord Steyne was standing near the fire. He laughed. "Dear little innocent lamb!" he said. "Can't the shepherd defend the lamb he owns?"

"The shepherd," answered Becky, laughing, "is too fond of playing cards and going out to play billiards."

Chapter 13
A family in need

Now it is time to find at what is happening to some friends in Chelsea. How is Amelia after the storm of Waterloo? What has happened to Major Dobbin, who used to visit the little cottage so often? And is there any news of the Collector of Boggley Wollah?

Let's take the last first. Our fat friend Joseph Sedley returned to India quite soon after his escape from Brussels. On the voyage, he saw Napoleon Bonaparte at St Helena, where the ex-emperor had just arrived. Jos talked on the ship as if he had already seen Napoleon at the battle of Waterloo. He certainly knew a lot about Quatre Bras and Waterloo. He knew the position of every regiment and how many men it had lost. He didn't say that he had *not* been there. He described what the Duke of Wellington did and said at every moment of the day, and it was clear that he must have been there, although, as a man who was not in the army, his name didn't appear in the reports. Perhaps in the end he made himself believe that he really took part in the battles. He certainly drew a great deal of interest in Calcutta, and he was called Waterloo Sedley during the whole of his stay in Bengal.

Jos's bankers in London had orders to pay one hundred and twenty pounds a year to his father and mother in Chelsea. It was the chief income of the old people, because all old Sedley's hopes of becoming rich again came to nothing. He tried to be a wine merchant, a coal merchant, an agent for this and an agent for that, without success.

Jos Sedley

Amelia had a war widow's pension of fifty pounds a year. And there was also an amount of five hundred pounds, Dobbin said, which was left in the agent's hands at the time of Osborne's death. Dobbin wanted to put this into government bonds to bring Amelia interest at eight per cent. Old Mr Sedley was strongly against this plan. He thought the major must be being dishonest about it, and he told Dobbin to show him Osborne's accounts immediately. When Dobbin went red in the face and was more awkward than ever, Mr Sedley was sure he was being dishonest with Amelia's money. At last Dobbin was angry.

"Come upstairs, sir," he said, "and I will show you." He took the old gentleman up to his bedroom and showed him George's accounts and a large number of pieces of paper that George had given – promises to pay money he owed. "You will see," Dobbin added, "that at the time of his death, George Osborne had less than a hundred pounds in the world. The five hundred pounds was made up by his fellow officers." The last was not true. Dobbin himself had given every penny of the money. He had also paid all the costs of burying his friend and bringing Amelia back to England.

"I'm sorry," the old man said. "I was quite wrong. Please forgive me."

The day came when Amelia had to send her son to school. She had taught him as much as she could. It was with great difficulty that she found the money to pay for the school, and to dress him for school in a way that was proper for the son of a great man like George Osborne. And it was very hard to let him go into the dangers of school, with cruel teachers and rough schoolfellows. Georgy himself ran off cheerfully to school and did very well there.

Amelia had forgotten all her husband's faults and failings. She remembered only the splendid and beautiful hero who had gone to fight, and die bravely for king and country. He was perfect, and so was the little boy, his son.

That is what Miss Osborne, old Mr Osborne's oldest daughter, thought too, when she saw him at the Dobbins' house. The major's sisters (perhaps by his orders) took notice of Amelia and her son, and that is how Georgy was visiting them when their friend Miss Osborne came to see the Misses Dobbin.

That night, when Georgy came home in the Dobbins' carriage, he had a fine gold watch and chain round his neck.

"There was an old lady. She cried and kissed me a lot. She said she's my aunt, but she isn't pretty. I don't like her. I like apples; I had a red one. I like you, mama. The old lady gave me the watch."

At dinner, Miss Osborne said to old Mr Osborne, "Oh, sir! I've seen little Georgy. He is beautiful – so beautiful! And just like *him*!"

The old man did not say a word. But he went very red, and his hands shook.

Chapter 14
Becky goes back to Queen's Crawley

Sir Pitt Crawley was very ill.

"We'll have to go to Queen's Crawley, my dear," said Mr Pitt in the Park Lane house that had been Miss Crawley's.

"Yes, dear," said Lady Jane.

At Queen's Crawley the old baronet had not many days to live. His son took charge of the place and looked at the accounts. The old man's accounts were "mixed up", as he had told Becky. Queen's Crawley needed to have a lot of money spent on it, but Pitt did not want to use his own money (the money that had been Miss Crawley's). "If he doesn't die," Pitt thought, "he could get things 'mixed up' again and lose my money." Perhaps Pitt also thought how many things he could do when his father died and he himself became baronet.

Early one morning, Pitt Crawley was working on the account books when there was a quiet knock on the door. The nurse came in. Sir Pitt was dead.

The new Sir Pitt wrote to Rawdon asking him and Becky to the burial.

The letter arrived at Curzon Street. Rawdon Crawley understood only half of Sir Pitt's long words and difficult sentences. "What's the good of going to that stupid place?" he thought. "I can't bear being alone with Pitt after dinner. And horses there and back will cost us twenty pounds."

But he took the letter – as he took all difficulties – to Becky. She read it, and jumped up, crying "Hurrah!"

"Hurrah?" said Rawdon. "The old man hasn't left us any money, Becky. I had mine when I was twenty-one. You don't really want to go, do you?"

"Of course we must go, you silly old man. I want your brother to give you a seat in Parliament. And there you will help Lord Steyne. And he will get you a post as Governor in the West Indies or somewhere."

So when the black clothes were ready, Colonel Crawley and his wife took their places in the coach. ("We don't want to look rich," said Becky, "so we'll use the public coach. You can sit beside the driver and talk about horses.")

At Queen's Crawley, Pitt bowed politely to Rebecca. But Lady Jane took both Rebecca's hands and kissed her. This brought tears to Becky's eyes – a most unusual thing, and even I don't know how she did it.

After dinner, Lady Jane and Becky spent half an hour together. By the end of that time, they were the best of friends, and Lady Jane told Sir Pitt later that Rebecca was a kind, open, friendly young woman. This opinion might have owed something to Becky's interest in Lady Jane's two children. Perhaps it was added to by her answer to Lady Jane's worry about Miss Crawley's punishment of Rawdon and Becky by giving all her money to Pitt:

"Dear Lady Jane, we don't care about being poor. I have been used to it since I was a child. And I am very glad that Miss Crawley's money is being used to bring back the splendour of a fine old family. I am so proud to be a member of that family. I am sure Sir Pitt will make a much better use of the money than Rawdon could."

When they left Queen's Crawley, Colonel and Mrs Rawdon Crawley were very good friends with Sir Pitt Crawley and his wife.

Chapter 15
More trouble for Amelia

Mr Osborne's lawyer came to Chelsea to see Amelia.

"Mr Osborne," the lawyer read from a letter, "offers to take the boy, George Osborne, and to leave him all his money when Mr Osborne dies. He will pay you, Mrs George Osborne, two hundred pounds a year. It must be understood that the child will live entirely with his grandfather, although you, Mrs George Osborne, will occasionally be allowed to see him here at your house."

The lawyer read the letter aloud and passed it to Amelia. She was very seldom angry, but on this occasion she stood up, tore the paper into a hundred pieces, dropped them on the floor and kicked them.

"So I am to take money to be separated from my child? Tell Mr Osborne that it is not the kind of letter a gentleman would write. It is not the kind of letter I expect from the father of a truly brave man like my husband. I will not answer it. I wish you good morning, sir. Please go!"

Amelia did not know then how much trouble the little family was in. It seemed that the money from Jos was not arriving. The fact was that Mr Sedley was getting very old, and his ideas were becoming more and more childish. One business after another failed. The money from Jos *was* arriving, but it went straight to a debt-collector to meet the old man's debts.

When at last Amelia learnt the truth, she knew that she was defeated. Her child must go from her – to others – to forget her. She must let him go. And then – and then she would go to George. She and George would watch over the boy, and wait for him until he came to them in heaven.

Amelia wrote to Miss Osborne. In simple words she told her the reasons for her decision.

My father has had more bad luck. My own money is too little to keep my parents and to give George the kind of life that he ought to have ...

With tears in her eyes, Miss Osborne showed the letter to her father.

"Ah!" he said. "So Mrs Pride has come down? Ha, ha! I knew she would." But he went to his desk, took a key from it, and threw it down in front of his daughter. "Get the room that used to be *his* ready," he said, between laughing and nearly crying. "And you can send that woman some money. Send her a hundred pounds."

"And I'll go and see her tomorrow?" Miss Osborne asked.

"Do what you like. But she doesn't come here, you understand. No, no, no! But she mustn't be in need now."

"Here is some money, father," Amelia said, kissing the old man and putting a note for a hundred pounds in his hand.

The widow told Georgy the news very carefully. She expected him to be broken-hearted over leaving her. He wasn't. The next day at school, he told the other boys proudly that he was going to be rich, and have a carriage and his own small horse, and go to a much finer school. "And when I'm rich, I'll buy Marker's pencil-case and pay the cake-woman."

Chapter 16
Becky in trouble

At last the day came when the debt-collectors caught Colonel Rawdon Crawley. They took him to Cursitor Street, and from there he wrote to Rebecca:

Dear Becky. They've got me in Cursitor Street. It's the debt to Nathan – a hundred and fifty pounds. Please get the seventy pounds in my desk and offer it to Nathan, and ask him to let me owe the rest. If he won't do it, please sell my watch and anything else. Love, R

The answer came a long time later:

Poor dear, I'm so sorry I couldn't come at once. I have a terrible headache, and the doctor won't let me leave my bed. As soon as I'm better – or before – I'll get you free. Love, Becky

Rawdon was worried. He remembered that Sir Pitt and Lady Jane were in London, and he sent a message asking if they could help him in some way.

Lady Jane herself came. "Pitt is at the Houses of Parliament," she said, "so I came."

The business of the debt was quickly settled. Rawdon thanked Lady Jane a hundred times. Then he hurried home to look after Becky. He ran some of the way, and he was breathing heavily when he reached his own house.

The windows of the sitting-room showed that the room was full of light. Becky had said that she was in bed, ill. Rawdon could not understand it. He took out his door-key and opened the front door. He could hear laughter in the sitting-room, and he went upstairs to it and opened the door.

A little table was ready with dinner and wine. Becky was sitting down in full evening dress with a great number of jewels. Lord Steyne had her hand in his, and he was laughing.

Becky jumped up with a cry when she saw Rawdon's white face at the door. There was a terrible look in his eyes, and she threw herself down in front of him.

"I am innocent, Rawdon!" she cried. "As God is my judge, I am innocent." And to Lord Steyne she said, "Tell him I am innocent."

Lord Steyne thought the colonel and his wife were trying to catch him. "You, innocent?" he cried. "You, innocent! When every jewel you are wearing was paid for by me? I have given you thousands of pounds, which this fellow has spent. You're as innocent as your mother, the dancing girl, and your husband the card-player."

Rawdon Crawley stepped quickly forward and struck Lord Steyne twice on the face with his open hand. "You lie, you dog!" he shouted. "You can send your friends tomorrow to arrange the duel. Take these jewels!" And he tore the rings and other jewels from Becky and threw them at Lord Steyne.

"Come upstairs," Rawdon said to his wife.

"Don't kill me, Rawdon," she said.

He laughed cruelly. "I want to see if that man is lying about the money. Has he given you any?"

"No," said Rebecca. "Or——"

"Give me your keys," Rawdon said.

Rebecca gave him all her keys except one. She hoped he might not notice that she hadn't given him that key. It was the key of a little desk which she kept in a secret place. But Rawdon found the desk, and Rebecca had to open it. It contained papers, jewels, love-letters many years old – and a small case containing bank-notes. Some of them were dated ten years before, and one was quite new, a note for a thousand pounds that Lord Steyne had given her.

"He gave you this, did he?" said Rawdon.

"Yes."

"I'll send it to him today," Rawdon said. "You might have let me have a hundred pounds out of all this, Becky!"

"I am innocent," Becky said again. And he left her without saying another word.

Sir Pitt was at home when Becky went to see him. He was looking at the newspaper, when she ran into the room where he was sitting.

It was clear that he had already heard all about the trouble in Curzon Street, because he looked at Becky with surprise and fear.

"Oh, don't look at me like that!" cried Becky. "I am innocent, Pitt. I don't seem innocent, but I swear I am. It's terrible. And just when everything I had worked for was happening – just when happiness was coming to us."

"Is this true that I see in the paper, then?"

"Yes, it's true," Becky said. "Lord Steyne told me on Friday. The Colonial Office told him yesterday that the order had been made. It was just what I had been asking Lord Steyne to arrange. I know I had money that Rawdon didn't know about. But *you* know how careless he is with money. You can understand why I didn't tell him about it."

Sir Pitt was looking less anxious.

Becky went on: "I did know that Lord Steyne liked me rather more than was proper. And I certainly tried to please him in every way an honest woman can. I thought I might get you, Pitt, made a lord. Lord Steyne and I talked about it. But the first thing I wanted was the post of Governor for Rawdon. I wanted it to be a surprise for him – when he saw it in the papers today. And now it has all gone wrong! Can you help me, Pitt, dear Pitt? Please!"

"I'm going to kill the fellow," Colonel Crawley told his friend Captain Macmurdo, "and I want you to arrange a meeting."

"Have you seen this in the newspaper?" Macmurdo asked. And he showed Rawdon a report:

> GOVERNOR OF COVENTRY ISLAND *A warship has just arrived from Coventry Island. The Governor, His Excellency Sir Thomas Liverseege, has died as a result of yellow fever. His loss is deeply felt in the island. The position of Governor is being offered to Colonel Rawdon Crawley, a well-known Waterloo officer.*

"I haven't heard anything about that," Rawdon said.

"It's a good job, Crawley. Three thousand a year, lovely island, excellent Government House. You can do what you like on the island. And a better job to follow it."

Sir Pitt Crawley met them. "You have seen the piece in the newspaper, then?" he said to Rawdon. And he tried hard to make Rawdon forgive Becky. But Rawdon was not ready to forgive her.

"She kept money hidden from me for ten years," he said. "She swore she hadn't got any from Steyne. As soon as I found it, she knew it was all over. I'll never see her again, Pitt. Never!"

There was no duel. Lord Steyne left England and did not return. The whole trouble was a closely guarded secret – a secret that was talked about all over London, and then all over England, and then all over the world, for a few weeks.

Poor Raggles in Curzon Street, the debt-collectors had him, and he spent years in prison.

And the pretty little lady who had lived in his house: where was she? Who cared? Was she really innocent or not? We all know how kind the world is. And if there was a doubt – we all know what Vanity Fair decides when there is a doubt.

Rawdon made arrangements for her to receive a fair income. And we know she was a woman who could make a little money go a long way. She never tried to see little Rawdon. He lived happily at Queen's Crawley, and he loved to read the newspapers and to see that in the *Coventry Island Gazette* the Governor was highly praised. (The *Coventry Island Herald* said that he was cruel and hard. The wife of the reporter on that paper had not been asked to a Government House party.)

The new Governor of Coventry Island didn't die of yellow fever until he had been four years on the island.

Chapter 17
Arrivals and departures

Old Sedley was sitting on a seat in the park. Amelia was beside him, and he was telling one of his stories that she had heard a hundred times. He did this often since he had got older and his wife had died. When she saw the little girl from the house next door coming running towards them, she jumped up. "Has something happened to Georgy?" she thought.

"He's come!" called the little girl. "Look!"

Amelia looked, and saw the tall figure of Dobbin coming across the grass. And of course she began to cry. She ran towards him and gave him both her hands. She wasn't changed. She was a little pale, but her eyes were the same, the kind trustful eyes. She smiled through the tears at his honest, well-remembered face. Why didn't he take her in his arms and swear that he would never leave her?

"I have another arrival to tell you about," he said.

"Mrs Dobbin?"

"Oh, no," he said. "There isn't a Mrs Dobbin. I mean your brother Jos. He came from India on the same ship with me. He has come home to make you all happy."

"Father!" Emmy cried. "Here's news! Jos is in England. He has come to take care of you."

I am afraid that the major stretched the truth a little in telling old Sedley that Jos had come home mainly to see his father.

Later, while the old man was half-asleep, Amelia had a long talk with Dobbin. It was all about her son, his wonderful beauty, his cleverness, and how well he was doing in his new school and at his new home in Russell Square.

The day arrived when Jos's carriage came and carried old Sedley and his daughter away from Chelsea. Emmy left nearly all her furniture to her good friends there. Just a few precious things were brought to their new home near Regent's Park. Among the precious things, Dobbin was glad to see a piano – *the* piano.

"I'm glad you've kept it," he dared to say to Emmy.

"Of course I've kept it. I value it more than anything I have in the world."

"Do you, Amelia?"

"Certainly. *He* gave it to me."

"I didn't know," said poor Dobbin.

She thought about that after he had gone. And then at last she knew that it was William who had given her the piano, not George. The pain was terrible.

Old Mr Sedley's last illness lasted for several months. Old Mr Osborne's was short, but before it he had changed his mind about Amelia.

Young George Osborne was very fond of Major Dobbin. And because of that, his grandfather, old Mr Osborne, saw Dobbin quite often. Mr Osborne's opinion of the soldier had changed completely since their meeting in Brussels. More than once, he asked the major about – about Mrs George Osborne. It was a subject on which the major could talk readily. He told Mr Osborne about her sufferings, about her continuing love of her husband.

"You don't know what she suffered, sir," said honest Dobbin, "and I hope you will be kind to her. If she took

63

your son away from you, she gave hers to you. I know how much you loved your George, and you may be sure she loved hers ten times more."

"You are a good fellow," was all the old man said.

One day, when old Mr Osborne was expected at the breakfast table, they found him still in his room, and in four days he was dead. Old Sedley had died two days earlier.

The lawyer read out Mr Osborne's last wishes – he had changed them not long before. Most of his money was left to George, with Major Dobbin to look after it while George was a boy. But five hundred pounds a year went to George's mother, "the widow of my dear son, George Osborne".

Chapter 18
In Europe

Jos Sedley became anxious again about his health, and he decided to visit towns in Europe whose waters were famous. These towns were drawing very many British people at the time, and Jos included in his party his sister Emmy and her son, George, who was on his summer holidays. Georgy's "uncle" Dobbin was not in the party, but he often came to the towns they were staying in – to see that George was all right.

At Pumpernickel, there was a great dance, with a room to one side for games of chance. Georgy Osborne was not allowed to go into this room, but when nobody was looking, of course he did. It was very exciting. He was watching one game when a pretty lady seemed to lose all her money. Part of her face was covered by a mask. She saw the boy looking at her, and she said, "Will you do me a kindness?" She took out a little bag which contained one gold coin, and she said, "Please play this for me. Put it on any number. You will have 'beginner's luck'."

Georgy laughed with pleasure and put the coin on number fifteen.

Number fifteen won. "Thank you," said the pretty lady.

They couldn't say anything else because Dobbin and Jos came looking for George. Dobbin led the boy away, but Jos stayed. He sat down beside the lady and started to play.

"You aren't playing to win, are you?" the lady said. "Nor do I. I play to forget – but I can't. I can't forget old times. Your little nephew is just like his father. But you haven't changed."

"Good heavens, who is it?" cried Jos, very worried.

"Have you forgotten me, Joseph Sedley?" She took off her mask.

Jos's voice could only just be heard as he said, "Mrs Crawley!"

"Rebecca," she said softly, putting her hand on his. "I'm staying at the Elephant Hotel. Ask for Madame de Raudon."

Becky had been moving from one place to another in Europe. To live on the three hundred pounds a year she had from Colonel Rawdon, she had to go to the places that English people went to. And after a time, somebody who knew her always arrived. Then the English people in that place started talking, and Becky had to move on. It was not a good life.

The day after the meeting at the play-table, Jos dressed even more splendidly than usual and went to the Elephant Hotel. It was not one of the best hotels. He and Becky had a long and very friendly talk. At the end of it, it was clear to Jos that Becky's heart had first learnt to beat for him; that George Osborne had certainly run after her – against her wishes – but that she had never stopped thinking of Jos.

"She hasn't a friend in the world," Jos told Amelia after that meeting. And that was just what was needed to make the soft-hearted Emmy want to help.

"Oh, the poor creature, how she has suffered!" Amelia said when she had heard the whole story from her brother.

"She was not always your friend," said Dobbin.

Emmy was angry – in a way we have only seen once before – and spoke sharply to him before walking out of the room. It was the end of everything for Dobbin. He did not come to dinner with Amelia, Jos, George – and Rebecca.

After dinner, George was at the window. "Hello!" he said. "There's Dob's little carriage, and they are carrying his bags out to it. Is he going anywhere?"

"Yes," said Emmy, "he's going on a journey."

"And when is he coming back?" Georgy wanted to know.

"He is ... is not coming back," answered Emmy.

"Not coming back!" cried Georgy, who really loved his "uncle" Dobbin. And he jumped up and ran out before they could stop him. They saw him from the window, jumping into the carriage and throwing his arms round the major's neck. William spoke to him and kissed him on the head, and the boy got out, tears streaming from his eyes.

The rich people were leaving Pumpernickel because it was time to move to a place by the sea. Jos's doctor, too, was going to Ostend for the sea air. He wanted Jos to go there – there was money to be made out of Jos's illnesses – but the move was only made when Rebecca offered to go to Ostend. Jos paid for her move.

At Ostend, Emmy was so kind to Becky that Becky's heart seemed to be softened.

"Listen to me, Amelia," said Becky, looking at her with something near to real kindness. "I want to talk to you. You are no more fit to live alone in this world than a baby in arms. You must have a husband, you fool. And one of the best men I ever saw has offered to marry you

It was the end of everything for Dobbin

time after time. You turned him away, you silly, heartless, thankless little creature!"

"I tried ... I tried my best to love him, Rebecca," said Amelia, "but I couldn't forget——" and she finished her sentence by looking up at the picture of George.

"Couldn't forget *him*!" cried Becky. "That self-centred, dishonest, common show-off! That stupid, heartless fool! I'll tell you, the fellow was tired of you, and he was not going to marry you if Dobbin hadn't made him keep his promise. George himself told me that. He used to laugh about you to me, and he made love to me the week after he married you."

"It isn't true! It isn't true!" cried out Amelia.

"Not true?" Becky said, still kindly. "Look at this, then, you fool." She took a piece of paper from her dress, opened it, and put it in Emmy's hands. "You know his writing. He wrote that to me – wanted me to run away with him – the day before he was shot. I wouldn't have gone. He was worthless!"

Emmy looked at the letter. It was the one that George had put in among Becky's flowers at the dance in Brussels.

Amelia's head dropped down, and for almost the last time in this story, she began to weep. Was she weeping because her god had been shown to be a false god? Or were they tears of gladness because there was nothing now to keep her from loving with all her heart?

Indeed she did not cry as much as Becky expected.

Rebecca comforted and kissed her – a most unusual action for Mrs Becky. She treated Emmy like a child, and patted her head.

"And now," Becky said, "let's get a pen and paper, and write to him to come at once."

"I ... I wrote to him this morning," Emmy said, her face very red.

Two mornings later, Amelia and Georgy went down to the landing-place. There was a very strong wind, and great waves were rolling in.

"Oh, I do hope he won't cross in this weather," Emmy said.

"Of course he will," Georgy said. "Look, mother, there's the smoke from the ship."

The weather was so bad that there were very few people at the landing-place. Hardly anybody saw the very tall man step on shore. He was met by a lady in a very wet hat and shawl, who disappeared into his big old coat, whispering something like, "... forgive – dear William – dear, dear, dearest friend – kiss ..." and other things, in the most foolish way.

Georgy danced round them as they went towards the house, and then he ran off to see about breakfast. In the passage, Emmy's hat and shawl flew off. She went to undo William's great coat, and ... We will, if you please, leave them now, and go with George, and look after breakfast for the major.

And Becky? The last news we had of her, she was living in Brussels. Jos Sedley was in Brussels too.

Questions

Questions on each chapter

1 1 Where were the girls coming from?
  2 Where did they go in the carriage?

2 1 Where was Joseph Sedley when Rebecca first saw him?
  2 Why had he come back to Europe? (Because . . .)
  3 Where had Joseph promised to take Amelia?

3 1 Which two families lived in Russell Square?
  2 Whose friend was Captain Dobbin?
  3 Who did not have supper with the rest of the party?

4 1 What do you notice about the note from Sir Pitt Crawley?
  2 Who was the man in dirty old clothes?
  3 What did Mr Crawley explain to Becky?

5 1 What was "the most important fact" about Miss Crawley?
  2 Which two people sat one on each side of Miss Crawley at dinner every night?

6 1 Why was Amelia glad that the war in Europe was over?
  2 What had happened to Mr Sedley's ship?

7 1 Who came to the Park Lane house every day?
  2 What did Sir Pitt want Rebecca to do?
  3 Why couldn't Rebecca do it?

8 1 Who had owned the piano before Dobbin bought it?
  2 Where did George and Amelia go after their marriage?
  3 Who came on the coach from London?

9 1 What was among Becky's flowers?
  2 Where did Becky put the piece of paper?
  3 Who sold Jos two horses?
  4 What happened to George?

10 1 Where did Becky get the presents for Miss Crawley?
  2 Who were married by Miss Crawley's orders?
  3 What was the "news" from England that helped the Crawleys?
  4 What was Rawdon and Becky's income?

11 1 Who had sent money to George?
  2 Who was the lady in the carriage?
  3 What did Amelia call her son?

12 1 Whose house did Rawdon and Becky rent?
  2 Why did Rawdon want to fight duels with some married men?
  3 Why did Becky want a sheepdog?

13 1 Why did they call Jos "Waterloo Sedley"?
  2 What lie did Dobbin tell to old Sedley?
  3 Who gave Georgy a watch?

14 1 Why did the Rawdon Crawleys go to Queen's Crawley?
  2 How did they travel there?

15 1 What was happening to the money from Jos?
  2 Which room did Miss Osborne prepare for George?

16 1 Who got Rawdon out of Cursitor Street?
  2 What did Rawdon do with the jewels Becky was wearing?
  3 What position was offered to Rawdon?
  4 What happened to Raggles?

17 1 Who were the two "arrivals"?
  2 Who were the two "departures"?
  3 What did Amelia find out about the piano?

18 1 What did Georgy do for the lady in the mask?
  2 Who told Amelia the truth about George?
  3 Why did Dobbin come back?

Questions on the whole story

These are harder questions. Read the Introduction, and think hard about the questions before you answer them. Some of them ask for your opinion, and there is no fixed answer.

1 Thackeray called *Vanity Fair* "a novel without a hero". Here are lists of some of the main people in the story. Can you give ONE reason, and an example, in each case for *not* calling the person a "hero" or a "heroine"? (Example: *Jos Sedley* was not brave. For example, he ran away from Brussels, leaving Amelia.)
   Heroes? a Lieutenant George Osborne;
   b Rawdon Crawley; c Dobbin
   Heroines? d Amelia Sedley; e Rebecca Sharp; f Miss Crawley

2 Now name ONE good point in each of the people named in Question 1, and give an example. (Example: *Jos Sedley* tried to be a good son. For example, he sent money to his parents when they needed it.)

3 What, in your opinion, was a the worst, and b the best thing that Becky did?

4 What is amusing or funny in these examples of Thackeray's writing?
   a "There was another reason for Rawdon and Becky to leave London and take the best rooms at the best hotel in Brighton. They had no money." (page 28)
   b "One day, Dobbin arrived in a carriage, bringing a wooden horse, a drum, and other warlike toys for little Georgy – who was hardly six months old." (page 45)
   c "The new Governor of Coventry Island didn't die of yellow fever until he had been four years on the island." (page 61)

5 "It is true that the Raggles's happy life was entirely destroyed by the Crawleys' use of his house, Raggles himself being sent to prison for debt. But *somebody* has to pay, even for gentlemen who live on nothing a year." – What, in your opinion, did Thackeray really think about such "gentlemen"?

New words

awkward
    not moving or acting easily;
    appearing to do things with
    difficulty

billiards
    a game played on a cloth-
    covered table with pockets
    into which the balls are hit

butler
    head manservant

cavalry
    soldiers who fought on
    horseback

coach
    a large carriage pulled by
    four horses, taking
    passengers inside and on
    top

companion
    a woman who (like Miss
    Briggs) was paid to help
    and be the friend of another

conscience
    an inner sense that tells us
    when an action is wrong

debt
    money that is owed; **in debt**
    = owing money to another
    person or other people

defeat
    beat; being beaten in war

duel
    a fight (with pistols, hand
    guns) to settle a quarrel

fashion
    rich people's way of
    dressing or behaving at a
    particular time; **fashionable**
    = in the latest fashion

governess
    a woman who lives in the
    home and educates the
    children of the family

imitate
    copy another person's way
    of behaving, speaking, etc

income
    the amount of money which
    a person receives every
    year

innocent
    not having done anything
    wrong

regiment
    a large group of soliders
    (1,000 or more) under the
    command of a **colonel**

staff
    the officers who help a
    general in his work of
    commanding a number of
    regiments